Angelina™
Ballerina

The Rose Fairy
Princess

PLEASANT
COMPANY
PUBLICATIONS™

"And again, Angelina!" called Miss Lilly.

Angelina danced onto the stage. This was her last chance to prove that she would make the very best Rose Fairy Princess in the exciting new ballet.

The Rose Fairy Princess

Angelina™
Ballerina

Published by Pleasant Company Publications
© 2003 Helen Craig Limited and Katharine Holabird
Based on the text by Katharine Holabird and the illustrations by Helen Craig
From the script by Barbara Slade

The Angelina Ballerina name and character and the dancing Angelina logo are trademarks of HIT
Entertainment PLC, Katharine Holabird, and Helen Craig. ANGELINA is registered in the U.K. and Japan.
The dancing Angelina logo is registered in the U.K.

Visit our Web site at www.americangirl.com and
Angelina's very own site at www.angelinaballerina.com

Printed in the United States of America

03 04 05 06 07 08 09 10 NGS 10 9 8 7 6 5 4 3 2

Angelina twirled and leaped gracefully across the floor. She was concentrating so hard on dancing that she didn't notice that the ribbon of one of her slippers had come undone! As Angelina began her final leap, she tripped on the ribbon and toppled over with a *thud*.

"Never mind, Angelina," giggled Priscilla Pinkpaws as she walked by with her twin sister, Penelope.

"After all," added Penelope, "you can always join the chorus of dancing flowers!"

Later that day, all the little ballerinas crowded around
Miss Lilly to hear the results of the audition.

Miss Lilly raised her clipboard in the air and said, "The
Rose Fairy Princess shall be danced by—"

"Oh, Miss Lilly!" Penelope interrupted. "I knew I'd get the part. I just knew it!"

"Penelope, darling," said Miss Lilly gently, "I am sorry, but this time, Angelina will dance the part of the Rose Fairy Princess. And you, Penelope, will make a beautiful dancing flower."

Angelina gasped, "You mean . . . I got the part?" She could hardly believe it was true!

As Angelina and Alice left the dressing room that
afternoon, Angelina chattered excitedly. "Oh, Alice, I got
the part! I'm going to practice every day. I'm going to be
the *best* Rose Fairy Princess—ever!"

Angelina twirled all the way down the long hall and found
Miss Lilly talking to the stage manager.

"A single wire!" exclaimed Miss Lilly. "What a perfect finale. My beautiful Rose Fairy Princess will fly across the stage on a single wire!" Then she noticed Angelina. "It's marvelous, don't you think, Angelina?"

But Angelina's stomach was doing flip-flops. "A single wire?" she whispered to herself. "Oh, no!"

"Miss Lilly?" Angelina began timidly. She held her tail to keep it from quivering. "I was just wondering if a single wire is such a good idea. The audience might see the wire, and . . . um . . . that could be a-a-a very big problem."

"A problem?" said Miss Lilly, holding up a beautiful pink tutu with wings.

"Yes! But a ladder . . . ," Angelina continued hopefully, "a tall ladder decorated with vines to look like a tower—that would be something!"

Miss Lilly didn't seem to be listening. She held the tutu in front of Angelina to check its size, then lifted the winged tutu into the air and said, "Oh, Angelina, just imagine the feeling of soaring above the stage like a bird. You will be magnificent!"

But Angelina wasn't so sure.

"Why, you're the bravest, most daring mouse I've ever known," said Alice, trying to comfort Angelina.

"But this is just one little wire!" Angelina exclaimed. "What if it breaks?"

"It won't break," Alice reassured her. "I'm sure that Miss Lilly . . ."

But something had caught Angelina's eye—a poster for the circus, featuring Zivo, the magnificent acrobat. He would be able to help!

Soon the mouselings were peeking through the flaps of a
colorful circus tent. "There he is!" said Angelina. "The
most daring trapeze artist in the world." Angelina grabbed
Alice's paw and pulled her into the tent.

"Mr. Zivo!" Angelina called, craning her neck to watch him as he sailed through the air on a trapeze. "Can you teach me to fly on a single wire?"

Zivo released his grip on the trapeze, did a magnificent triple flip, and landed on the ground beside Angelina.

"A single wire?" he asked. "Little mouseling, you've come to the right place. Follow me!" He led Angelina toward the huge ladder in the center of the ring.

Angelina climbed the ladder, which seemed to stretch on forever. Finally she stepped onto a tiny platform near the top of the tent. She strapped on a harness and then reached out to touch the hook that Zivo had lowered for her. The hook felt shaky and fragile.

"Oh," Angelina whimpered. "I can't do it." She suddenly felt dizzy. Before she could fasten the hook to her harness, Angelina lost her balance and fell down, down, down . . . *Plunk!* She bounced three times before settling into a tangled heap in the middle of the safety net.

Alice had been watching from the stands, and she rushed to the net. "Oh, Angelina," Alice said kindly. "Maybe it's not so bad being a dancing flower after all."

That afternoon at rehearsal, Angelina danced her part
nervously, dreading the moment when she would have to
face the single wire. Then, she had an idea. She clasped her
hand against her forehead and swayed across the stage.
She spun around once and landed on the floor in a faint.

"Angelina," Miss Lilly said gently, "are you alright?"

"Oh, dear," Angelina said in her weakest voice. "I must have fainted."

"She probably won't be able to dance the part, Miss Lilly!" Penelope piped up from the circle of dancers. "But I can! I know every step!"

"Thank you, Penelope," said Miss Lilly as she helped Angelina sit up. "But I'm sure Angelina will be alright. My little Rose Fairy Princess just needs her rest."

On the evening of the performance, Alice handed Angelina
a small gift.

"It's for good luck," Alice said. "I mean, not that you'll
need it," she added quickly.

Angelina opened the box and found a delicate little bird attached to a thin wire. She smiled as she watched the bird swing back and forth on the wire. But then—*snap!* The wire broke!

"Oh, Alice," Angelina said. "What am I going to do?"

"I don't know," replied Alice. "I wish I could do something. I'd even fly across the stage for you if I could."

Angelina threw her arms around Alice. "That's it!" she cried. "You'll fly across the stage instead of me. We'll switch costumes right before the finale, and no one will ever know!"

In front of a large audience that evening, Angelina danced the part of the Rose Fairy Princess beautifully. As the grand finale approached, she disappeared behind the scenery and motioned to Alice, who was still dancing onstage. "Now, Alice!" Angelina whispered urgently.

Alice tiptoed away from the line of dancing flowers and made her way toward Angelina in the dim light backstage.

"I'm coming, Angelina!" she called. But then her costume snagged on a nail at the back of the Rose Fairy castle. Alice struggled furiously, trying to free herself, but it was no use!

The applause ended and the music for the next scene began. "Alice?" Angelina called into the darkness. Where was her friend?

As the curtains parted, Angelina knew what she had to do. She took a deep breath. "I won't let you down, Miss Lilly," she said, slipping her arms into the harness. "After all, I am the Rose Fairy Princess!"

As she was lifted into the air, Angelina's fear gave way to excitement, and then pure joy! She soared through the air, high above the dancing flowers. The audience leaped to their feet and applauded. Angelina felt magnificent, just as Miss Lilly had said she would.

The next day, Angelina hung her little bird in her bedroom window.

"You were a wonderful dancing flower," she said to Alice, who was mending her torn costume.

"Do you really think so?" Alice asked, beaming.

"Yes," said Angelina. "And you know what? I'm going to talk to Miss Lilly about doing a ballet about a circus girl." Angelina gave the little bird a gentle push. "A dancing circus girl who flies across the stage on a single wire!" she added.

"But, Angelina . . ." Alice said in a worried voice.

"I'll play the circus girl," Angelina continued. "And it will be the best ballet ever!"